Violet
the Painting
Fairy

Special thanks to Narinder Dhami

ISBN 978-0-545-70833-3

All rights reserved. Published by Scholastic Inc., 557 Broadway, New York, NY 10012, by arrangement with Rainbow Magic Limited.

12 11 10 9 8 7 6 5 4 3 2 1   15 16 17 18 19 20/0

Printed in the U.S.A.   40

This edition first printing, March 2015

The Fairyland
Palace

Bridge

Sara Sketchley's
house

Rainspell

Island

Maze

Park

Carrie's
Jewelry
Shop

Beach and
Boardwalk

Violet
the Painting
Fairy

by Daisy Meadows

SCHOLASTIC INC.

I'm a wonderful painter—have you heard of me?
Behold my artistic ability!
With palette, brush, and paints in hand,
I'll be the most famous artist in all the land!

The Magical Crafts Fairies can't stop me!
I'll steal their magic, and then you'll see
That everyone, no matter what the cost,
Will want a painting done by Jack Frost!

Contents

Paint Problems

"We're not far from the lighthouse now, Kirsty," said Rachel Walker. The best friends were walking along the cliff toward the Rainspell Island Lighthouse. "Dad said we can't miss it! I wonder what he meant?"

"We'll find out soon!" Kirsty Tate

replied. "I'm so glad we came to Rainspell for another vacation, Rachel. There's no other place like it in the whole world!"

The girls were spending their spring break on Rainspell Island. They were taking turns staying with Kirsty's mom and dad at their bed and breakfast one night, and then with Rachel's parents at the campsite the next night.

"Plus, it's an extra-special vacation because it's Rainspell Crafts Week," Rachel pointed out. "*And* because of our adventures with the Magical Crafts Fairies!"

When the girls arrived on Rainspell

Island a few days earlier, Kayla the Pottery Fairy had invited them to Fairyland, where a Crafts Week was also taking place. Kayla and the other Magical Crafts Fairies were organizing the event. Kayla told the girls that King Oberon and Queen Titania would choose the most beautiful crafts, and use them to decorate their royal palace.

But as the queen welcomed everyone to Crafts Week, Jack Frost and his goblins had hurled paint-filled balloons into the crowd! The Magical Crafts Fairies and even Queen Titania herself had been splattered with bright green paint. In all the chaos and confusion, Jack Frost and his goblins had stolen the Magical Crafts Fairies' special objects. They were the source of the fairies' powerful magic!

Jack Frost had declared that he was the best artist ever, and he'd taken the magic objects to ensure that no one else could ever outdo him. As everyone watched helplessly, Jack Frost had magically whisked himself and the goblins away, to hide the objects in the human world. The fairies had been horribly upset, but Rachel and Kirsty stepped forward right away to offer their help. The girls were determined to prevent crafts everywhere from turning into complete disasters!

"Thank goodness we already found Kayla's vase, Annabelle's pencil sharpener, Zadie's thimble, and Josie's ribbon," Kirsty said. "I really enjoyed our pottery, drawing, sewing, and jewelry-making workshops."

"Me, too," Rachel agreed. "But they would have been totally ruined if the fairies hadn't gotten their magic objects back just in time!"

Kirsty nodded. "I can't wait to try Polly Painterly's class at the lighthouse today," she said eagerly. "Painting is one of my favorite things!"

"But what do you think the class will be like, now that Violet the Painting Fairy's magic paintbrush is missing?" Rachel asked anxiously.

"Well, as Queen Titania always says, we have to wait for the magic to come to us and see!" Kirsty reminded her.

Suddenly, Rachel spotted the lighthouse up ahead of them.

"Now I see what Dad meant when he said we couldn't miss it!" She laughed. The lighthouse was painted in bold blue and white stripes, and the top was bright red.

"I read in the Crafts Week pamphlet that Polly Painterly is the lighthouse keeper, and a famous local artist, too," Kirsty said as they walked up to the colorful building.

"She must be pretty busy, then!" Rachel remarked. There was a sign taped to the door—PAINTING CLASS IN

THE LANTERN ROOM TODAY. The girls
went inside and began climbing the
spiral staircase up to the very top. The
walls were lined with pretty watercolor
paintings of Rainspell Island, all signed
Polly Painterly.

"These are beautiful," Kirsty said.

"Look, Rachel, this is the forest where we met Ruby the Red Fairy." She pointed at one of the paintings.

"Our very first fairy adventure!" Rachel said with a smile.

The first thing Rachel and Kirsty noticed when they reached the lantern room at the top of the lighthouse was the stunning view. Through the enormous window that ran all the way around the circular room, they could see sailboats bobbing on the sea, golden beaches backed by white cliffs, the village of little cottages, and the rolling countryside.

In the room, a group of kids wearing painting smocks were standing behind easels, waiting for the class to start. Meanwhile, a woman with bright pink streaks in her blonde hair was handing out palettes, brushes, and tubes of paint.

"Hi, girls," the woman called. "I'm Polly Painterly. Come and join us!"

"I'm Kirsty, and this is Rachel," Kirsty explained, noticing that there were lots more paintings propped along the walls of the lantern room.

"We were just admiring the view!"

"Wonderful, isn't it?" Polly sighed happily. "It inspires all my work." She gave the girls some painting materials and smocks to protect their clothes, then clapped her hands for silence.

"Welcome to Rainspell Lighthouse," Polly said. "I can't wait to show you all how much fun painting can be!

First, we're going to mix up some colors. Let's start with yellow and blue, then we'll try yellow and red. Can anyone guess what colors those will make?"

"Yellow and blue make green," Kirsty said, remembering something she'd learned in school.

"And yellow and red make orange," a boy next to Rachel added.

Polly showed everyone how to squeeze the paints onto their palettes and mix them with their brushes. But Kirsty was horrified to see that her yellow and blue mixture ended up a sludgy gray color, not green at all! Then she tried swirling the yellow and red paint together, but that turned gray, too.

"This is awful!" Rachel groaned, making a face. "All I get is gray!"

The other kids were having the same problem. Polly looked bewildered. "Try mixing red and white," she suggested. "You should get pink."

Everyone did what she said, but once again all the mixtures turned a dull gray! The paint was also very thin. It began to dribble off the palettes onto the floor, making a complete mess.

"Why is everything going wrong?" Polly wondered aloud, frowning. The

girls glanced knowingly at each other.
This was all because of Jack Frost!

"It must be a bad batch of paint," Polly
decided. "I'll grab some more and clean
all the brushes, too. While I'm gone, take
a look at my paintings to get some ideas
for your own work." Clutching the dirty
brushes, she disappeared down the spiral
staircase.

"What a disaster, Kirsty," Rachel whispered as they studied a painting of a sailboat. "As long as Violet's magic paintbrush is missing, our paintings will be terrible!"

Kirsty peered closely at Polly's painting. "Rachel," she whispered, her voice full of excitement, "see that strange, glowing light on the tip of the sail?"

"What is it?" Rachel breathed, her eyes wide.

As the girls watched, the light headed directly toward them! Then it transformed into a little fairy, who fluttered right out of the painting.

"It's Violet!" Kirsty whispered, grabbing Rachel's arm. "Violet the Painting Fairy!" Kirsty hoped she had news about her missing paintbrush.

Amazing Artist

Rachel and Kirsty moved closer together to hide Violet from the other kids as she flew toward them. The little fairy winked. She was dressed in rolled-up overalls, a colorful striped top, and purple boots. Her dark ponytail was held in place with a tiny paintbrush.

"Hello, girls,"
Violet whispered.
"As you already
know, yellow and
blue should *not* make
gray! All my beautiful
paint colors are ruined
now that Jack Frost has my
magic paintbrush. Will you help me
get it back?"

"Of course we will!" Rachel said right
away. Violet beamed at the girls, but
then a look of alarm crossed her face.
The other kids were making their way
toward the sailboat painting. Without
another word, Violet dove headfirst into
the pocket of Kirsty's smock and
disappeared from view.

"I really like this painting," said one of

the boys. "The ocean looks so real."

"It's almost like you could dive right into the waves," Kirsty agreed.

"Polly's paintings are amazing," another girl said. "I love this one of the beach in winter."

"Me, too," said Rachel.

"Give me a break!" a scornful voice piped up behind them. "Polly's paintings aren't so great. I can paint a million times better than that!"

Everyone spun around in surprise. Kirsty and Rachel saw a boy wearing a long smock and a baseball cap standing at an easel on the other side of the room. He twirled his paintbrush expertly in one hand, glaring at Kirsty, Rachel, and the others.

"Really?" Rachel asked. "Prove it! Can we see your painting?"

The boy shrugged. "I just started," he replied. "But sure, come and watch a painting genius at work!"

Rachel and Kirsty went over to his easel, followed by the other kids. The boy's canvas was almost blank, except for a blue streak at the top. But as everyone watched his confident brushstrokes, the painting began to take shape. Rachel quickly realized that the boy was doing a self-portrait, with the seashore in the background.

"This painting is incredible!" Rachel murmured to Kirsty as the boy added some seagulls flying through the clouds. "You can almost see each grain of sand."

"And the waves look like they're rolling right off the canvas," Kirsty added. The only strange thing was that the boy had painted himself with *very* big feet! Kirsty glanced down and gasped when she saw the boy's big feet under the easel.

"You must be gasping with amazement at my wonderful painting!" the boy said smugly.

"Oh—yes!" Kirsty said. She nudged Rachel. "Look at his feet," she whispered to her friend. "He's not green, but I think he might be a goblin!"

Then Rachel noticed something,

too—a few strands of long, icy hair
poking out of the top of the boy's smock.

"It's not a goblin, Kirsty," Rachel
whispered back. "It's Jack Frost!"

Just then, Kirsty felt a tiny hand
tugging on her sleeve.

"Jack Frost is using my magic

paintbrush to paint his picture!" Violet whispered indignantly. Kirsty looked a little closer and saw a faint haze of shimmering magic around the brush.

At that moment, Polly Painterly hurried back into the room. "I have new paint and clean brushes for everyone," she announced.

The other kids rushed over to collect their new materials. Meanwhile, Kirsty and Rachel stayed behind to confront Jack Frost.

"We know you have Violet the Painting Fairy's magic brush!" Kirsty said, looking at him sternly. "She'd like it back, please."

"No way!" Jack Frost declared with an icy sneer. "I love painting pictures, especially of myself. I have a wonderful gallery of self-portraits back at my Ice Castle. I plan to paint many, many more. No pesky fairies or silly human girls are going to stop me!"

Clutching the paintbrush, he dodged around the girls and ran away down the spiral staircase.

"Quick, Kirsty!" Rachel said urgently. "We can't let him get away!"

A Frosty Gallery

The girls quickly slipped out of the lantern room. No one noticed, because Polly was still giving out new painting supplies to the other kids.

"It might be faster if Violet turns us into fairies." Kirsty panted as they hurried down the stairs.

"Great idea," Violet agreed. Suddenly, they heard a familiar voice below them call, "Hello, girls!" Rachel and Kirsty glanced down and saw Artie Johnson, the Crafts Week organizer, walking up the winding stairs. With a squeak of alarm, Violet darted down into Kirsty's pocket again.

"Hi, Artie," said Rachel as both girls stopped to let her pass. Jack Frost was getting away, Rachel realized, but there was nothing they could do just then.

"We're really enjoying Crafts Week," Kirsty added.

Artie beamed at them. "I'm glad to hear it," she replied. "I'm also glad to see that *some* kids, like you, have nice manners—unlike that rude boy who just pushed past me!"

Kirsty and Rachel glanced at each other. *Jack Frost!*

"I'm here to check on the painting class," Artie went on. "You're not leaving already, are you?"

Rachel thought fast. "We'll be back in a little while," she replied. "We just remembered that we, um, have something important to do first."

"See you later," Artie said, heading up to the lantern room. The girls could see the rest of the spiral staircase below them, but Jack Frost had disappeared.

"What now?" Kirsty asked, dismayed, as Violet popped out of her pocket.

"Remember what Jack Frost said about the art gallery at his Ice Castle?" Rachel recalled. "Maybe he went there."

"It's worth a try!" Violet agreed. With one twirl of her

wand, she transformed the girls into tiny winged fairies. Then Violet waved her wand one more time, and a cloud of dazzling sparkles whirled them all away to Jack Frost's Ice Castle.

A few seconds later, Violet, Rachel, and Kirsty found themselves in Jack Frost's art gallery. It was a gigantic room. The frozen walls were crammed with paintings in frames of carved ice. All the  paintings were of Jack Frost in different poses! There were palettes, blank canvases, and tubes of paint lying all around the room.

"Look—there he is!" Kirsty whispered as the three friends landed on top of one of the picture frames.

Jack Frost was seated on a stool in front of an easel in the middle of the room. He had Violet's magic paintbrush in his hand! He was painting another picture of himself, this time sitting on his ice throne. A group of goblins, wearing green smocks and berets, were busy framing and hanging the paintings all around the room.

Rachel looked down and noticed that there was a big pile of paintings still waiting to be framed. Some goblins nearby were chipping away at blocks of ice, carving the frames as fast as they could.

"These paintings are boring!" one of the goblins complained to the others. "They're all of Jack Frost! Why won't he paint any pictures of *us*?"

"He says we're not handsome enough!" another goblin grumbled.

"Jack Frost won't let us try the magic paintbrush, either," said the goblin next to him. "He's so mean!"

The goblins' conversation gave Kirsty an idea! She whispered to Rachel and Violet, and the three of them flew out of the gallery into the empty hallway.

"The goblins have a lot of work to do," Kirsty pointed out, her eyes twinkling. "I think they need some help! Violet, could you disguise me and Rachel as goblins?"

Violet frowned. "Yes, but you know I don't have all my magic powers without my paintbrush," she replied. "And goblin disguises use a whole lot of magic! I'm not sure how long the disguises will last."

"We'll be quick," Kirsty promised. "I think I know how we can get the paintbrush back!"

Violet nodded. She waved her wand, surrounding the girls with a magical ring of sparkles.

The girls had been disguised as goblins before, but Kirsty was still shocked when she looked down at her hands and saw them becoming bright green! Rachel was turning the same shade of green. Her nose, ears, and feet were growing bigger, too. Kirsty felt her own nose and ears—they were *enormous*!

"You both look very goblin-like!"

Violet giggled as the girls hurried back into the gallery. "Good luck!"

"I keep tripping over my feet!" Rachel murmured as she and Kirsty headed over to Jack Frost. He was just about to begin a new painting.

"Should I clean your brush before you get started?" Kirsty offered. But Jack Frost didn't even look at her.

"Get me a fresh jar of water," he ordered. Rachel ran off to grab it.

"What about your brush?" asked Kirsty. "It looks awfully dirty."

"I'm out of blue paint," Jack Frost snapped, throwing the empty tube on the floor. "Bring me some immediately!"

Kirsty dug through the nearest pile of paints and found a tube of blue. Jack Frost snatched it from her, then grabbed the water from Rachel.

"I could clean your brush quickly while you decide what to paint," said Rachel innocently.

Jack Frost ignored her. He dunked the magic paintbrush in the water, squeezed the blue paint onto his palette, and began painting with swift, sure strokes. The girls exchanged looks of frustration.

"You know, your brush really needs a good cleaning—" Kirsty began.

"Get me some white paint!" Jack Frost shouted, still clutching the paintbrush tightly. "I have to finish this painting!"

For the next ten minutes, Jack Frost sent the girls on different errands while he painted a picture of himself in the Ice Castle gardens. To their dismay, he ignored all of their offers to clean his paintbrush.

At last, Jack Frost sighed in relief. "Finished!" he announced. For the first time, he glanced up at Kirsty and Rachel, and his icy brows drew together in a scowl.

"And who are you?" Jack Frost snarled suspiciously.

With a sinking heart, Kirsty glanced down at her hands. The bright green color was fading. Violet's magic was wearing off!

"Goblins!" Jack Frost howled furiously to the goblins across the room. "Lock up these pesky fairies in the dungeons *immediately*!"

Rainbow Fairies

As the goblins charged toward them,
Rachel grabbed a big armful of paint
tubes.

"Help me, Kirsty!" she cried.

"You don't have time to paint a
picture!" Jack Frost sneered. "You're
under arrest!" But realizing what Rachel
had planned, Kirsty scooped up a pile of

paints, too. Then the girls pulled the tops off the tubes and began squirting paint at the goblins! Blobs of yellow, blue, and red paint flew through the air, splattering the goblins from head to toe. The goblins stopped in their tracks. Then they all burst out laughing.

"Paint fight! Paint fight!" they hollered gleefully. Grabbing handfuls of the tubes, they began squirting paint at one another and whooping with joy.

"I order you to capture those silly fairies!" Jack Frost yelled as the girls flew toward the door. The goblins were having way too much fun to listen to him! Paint flew in all directions. Rachel could see that the gallery floor was already covered in streaks of different colors—red, orange, yellow, green, blue, indigo, and violet.

"The floor looks like a rainbow," Rachel said to Kirsty as they hurried out into the hallway where Violet was waiting.

"Yes—it's the same colors as the seven

Rainbow Fairies," Kirsty agreed. Then
she clapped a hand to her mouth in
excitement. "Rachel, that's *exactly* who
we need to help us get the magic
paintbrush back!"

"I was thinking the same thing!"
Rachel said as Violet flew to join them.
The girls quickly explained their idea,
and a happy smile lit up Violet's face.
"Fairyland, here we come!" she declared.

As they flew toward the hall window, Kirsty and Rachel heard Jack Frost yell at the goblins, "Stop this nonsense RIGHT NOW!"

The girls grinned and followed Violet out of the Ice Castle into the dark, frozen countryside.

A little while later, the three friends reached the blue skies and warm sunshine of Fairyland. Below, Kirsty and Rachel could see the pink towers of the royal palace, the toadstool houses, and the winding river.

As they swooped lower, they spotted the Rainbow Fairies in one of the wildflower meadows. Kirsty noticed that the fairies were playing a jump-rope game.

"Look at their colorful jump rope!"

Kirsty exclaimed. "It looks like a rainbow when it swings around."

Fern the Green Fairy and Amber the Orange Fairy held the ends of the rope and turned it, while the other five fairies skipped together, singing:

We're the Rainbow Fairies,
Colorful as can be,
Colors here, colors there,
Rainbow colors everywhere!

Suddenly, Ruby the Red Fairy glanced up and spotted them.

"It's Violet, Rachel, and Kirsty!" Ruby called. The other Rainbow Fairies looked up, too, and immediately got caught up in their jump rope. Laughing, the fairies untangled themselves and rushed to greet Violet and the girls.

"Rainbow Fairies, we really need your help," Rachel said. She quickly explained what had happened at Jack Frost's Ice Castle.

"Will you come?" Kirsty added.

"Try and stop us!" declared Inky the Indigo Fairy with a wide smile.

Color
Confusion

Violet, Rachel, and Kirsty led the way
back to the Ice Castle with the Rainbow
Fairies flying close behind. They all
slipped through the hall window. Then
Rachel, Kirsty, and Violet peeked into
the gallery.

"What a mess!" Rachel whispered.

The goblins were still running around, squirting paint at one another. They were all covered in streaks of different colors, from their heads to their giant feet. The floor was covered with puddles of paint, and some of the goblins were sliding around in it.

In the middle of the chaos, Jack Frost sat hunched over his easel. He was working on a new painting, and Kirsty could see that this one was bigger than

any of the others. She felt a little sorry
for Jack Frost! He was trying so hard to
ignore the goblins as he concentrated on
his picture.

"I told you all before," Jack Frost

shouted as a blob of
green paint flew by
his ear, "you'd
better not ruin any
of my precious
paintings—or you'll
be in big trouble!"
Silently, Violet
pointed at Jack Frost's
easel and waved to the other fairies.
Rachel, Kirsty, and the Rainbow Fairies
flew across the room, dodging the flying
paint and staying out of sight. They all
hid behind the easel.

"I need that special shade of ice blue to paint my cape," Jack Frost muttered, rummaging through the tubes of paint lying next to him.

Hearing this gave Rachel an idea. She whispered her plan to the others, and the Rainbow Fairies nodded, holding their wands in the air.

"Get ready," Ruby the Red Fairy whispered. "One, two, THREE!"

On the count of three, all of the Rainbow Fairies waved their wands. Glittering clouds of rainbow-colored fairy dust billowed around the room.

"Look at the paintings, Kirsty!"
Rachel said with a smile.

The pictures on the walls were changing color before their very eyes. A painting of an orange sunset had turned green, and a painting of the deep blue sea had become bright red. In the paintings Jack Frost had been working on earlier, his ice throne was now purple, and his Ice Castle was bright pink.

But Kirsty and Rachel could see that the biggest change was in the portraits of Jack Frost himself.

"Ha, ha, ha!" one of the goblins chuckled, suddenly noticing the painting closest to him. "See how funny Jack Frost looks in this picture? He has a green nose and orange hair! Ha, ha, ha!"

The other goblins stopped squirting

paint and stared curiously at the
paintings around them.

"His beard is indigo colored, and his
cape is bright red instead of icy blue,"
another goblin said with a grin.

"Look at this painting of him with his
wand!" a third goblin pointed out. "His
magic ice bolts are
daffodil-yellow—ha!"

Jack Frost looked more
upset by the minute.
"Stop that!" he
shrieked as the
goblins rolled
around on the
floor, laughing
hysterically and
getting covered in
even more paint.

"You'll pay for this, you giggling goofballs!"

When Violet gave the signal, all the fairies fluttered out from behind the easel. Jack Frost was so shocked, he almost fell off his stool.

"The Rainbow Fairies will change the colors of your paintings back to how they should be," Rachel told him. "But only if you return the magic paintbrush to Violet right away!"

Picture Perfect

Jack Frost's face fell.

"I'm not giving up the magic paintbrush!" he snapped. But as the goblins laughed themselves silly, wheezing and gasping for breath, Jack Frost frowned.

"Are you sure?" Violet asked him, her eyes twinkling.

Jack Frost groaned. "Fine. Here, take

it!" he mumbled, thrusting the paintbrush at Violet. The instant her fingers touched the handle of the brush, it shrank to its tiny Fairyland size. The girls and the Rainbow Fairies applauded happily.

"Finally!" Violet sighed with relief, waving the paintbrush in the air like a wand.

"Don't forget your end of the bargain!" Jack Frost reminded her.

Rachel and Kirsty watched as the seven Rainbow Fairies waved their wands to create sparkling magic once again. Showers of rainbow fairy dust

transformed the paintings back to their
true colors! The goblins stopped laughing
and picked themselves up off the floor.

"And this is for you," Violet told them
with a smile. She pointed her wand at an
empty spot on the
gallery wall, and
suddenly a new
framed painting
appeared. The
girls grinned at
one another when
they saw that it
was a painting of
three goblins! The
goblins squealed
with joy.

"Nonsense!" Jack Frost snorted, but
Kirsty thought he looked secretly happy.

"Girls, thank you again," Violet said as the fairies all left the gallery. "I really didn't think we were *ever* going to get my paintbrush away from Jack Frost!"

"We couldn't have done it without the Rainbow Fairies," Kirsty pointed out.

"We make a great team!" Sky the Blue Fairy said with a laugh.

"It's time for us all to return to Fairyland," Violet went on, "and you girls have a painting class to get to!" She raised her wand. "Good-bye, girls.

Thank you for being such loyal friends!"

"Good-bye," called the Rainbow
Fairies as Kirsty and Rachel were swept
away in a whirl of fairy magic.

Seconds later, the girls found themselves
back in the Rainspell Lighthouse,
standing by the spiral staircase outside
the lantern room. They hurried inside,
and found that the class was just about to
start again.

"I'm really looking forward to seeing all of your paintings," Artie was saying to the others.

"Me, too," agreed Polly Painterly. "Now, let's all try mixing those colors together again."

This time the painting class got off to a great start. Everyone, including Rachel and Kirsty, mixed beautiful shades of green, orange, and pink. As they began painting, Polly and Artie walked around the easels, giving everyone advice. Rachel decided to paint a view of the beach, but Kirsty wanted to try something different.

"Kirsty, that's a wonderful painting!"
Polly exclaimed a little later. Kirsty had
painted a portrait of Rachel with a
shimmering rainbow overhead.

"It's really good, Kirsty,"
Rachel said admiringly,
leaning over to
take a look.

"You know,
you should
enter your
painting in the
competition on
the last day of
Crafts Week,"
Artie told Kirsty.
"That rainbow looks incredibly
realistic—the colors glow!"

The girls glanced at each other.

"The rainbow reminds me of our fairy friends," Kirsty whispered as Artie walked away. "I'm just so glad we were able to help Violet today. And wasn't it great to see the Rainbow Fairies again?"

Rachel nodded. "I wonder which fairy will need our help tomorrow!" she said eagerly.

Kirsty grinned. She didn't know, but she knew one thing — it would be a magical adventure!

RAINBOW magic™

THE MAGICAL CRAFTS FAIRIES

Rachel and Kirsty have found Kayla,
Annabelle, Zadie, Josie, and Violet's
missing magic objects. Now it's time
for them to help

Libby
the Writing Fairy!

Join their next adventure
in this special sneak peek. . . .

Scattered Stories

"I wish I could paint like you, Kirsty!"
Rachel said, holding up her friend's
picture to admire it. The two girls had
gone to a painting workshop at
Rainspell Lighthouse the day before.
"Mom, don't you think this painting is
really good?"

Mrs. Walker was sitting in a chair outside their tent, soaking up the sunshine. She smiled and nodded. "You're very talented, Kirsty," Mrs. Walker declared, holding up the canvas to take a closer look. "You got Rachel's hair and eye color exactly right, and that rainbow arching over her head looks beautiful."

"Thanks!" Kirsty laughed. "Artie Johnson, the Crafts Week organizer, told me I should enter it in the competition tomorrow."

"And she also said you needed to choose a title for it," Rachel reminded her.

"How about *Rachel Under a Rainbow*?" suggested Mr. Walker. He was also seated outside the tent, reading a book.

"Perfect!" said Kirsty, and Rachel grinned. The girls were spending spring break on Rainspell Island with their parents, and they were having the best time ever. It was Crafts Week on Rainspell, so every day there were different activities for the girls to try. The Tates were staying at a b and b in the village, while the Walkers had rented a large tent on the campground. Rachel and Kirsty were taking turns spending one night at the b and b, and then the next at the campsite.

"Whenever I look at your painting, it reminds me of when we met the Rainbow Fairies right here on Rainspell Island, Kirsty," Rachel whispered.

"Me, too," Kirsty whispered back. "I'll never forget our first fairy adventure!"

"Girls, are you going to a Crafts Week workshop today?" called Mrs. Walker.

"Yes, Mom, but we haven't decided which one yet," Rachel replied.

"I think there might be a writing workshop this morning," Kirsty said. "One of the other kids in the painting class mentioned it yesterday."

"Maybe we could write a story about the Rainbow Fairies and take it to the workshop," Rachel whispered. "No one would ever guess it was true!"

"Great idea," Kirsty agreed.

The girls sat on the grass with pens and paper and began to scribble down their ideas.

"It all started when we both came to Rainspell on vacation and met on the boat," Rachel murmured.

"I thought we met in the village,"
Kirsty said, frowning.

Rachel thought for a minute and shook
her head. "No, I don't think so," she
replied. "Then we rescued Fern the
Green Fairy from the pot of gold."

"But we saw the rainbow first," Kirsty
reminded her.

Rachel felt confused. "Did we?" she
asked. "I don't remember that."

"Wasn't it Ruby the Red Fairy we
rescued from the pot?" Kirsty wondered.
"Or was it Sunny the Yellow Fairy?"

RAINBOW magic

These activities are magical!
Play dress-up, send friendship notes, and much more!